AFTER TONIGHT

A SLEIGH THE NIGHT PREQUEL

LADY MARIE

Cover design by Lady Marie

Editing by A.K. Edits

Formatting by Lady Marie

CONTENTS

TROPES, CONTENT WARNINGS + MORE

After Tonight is an Black erotic novella that takes places over the span of thirty-six hours in the fictional city of Oakwood, Maryland. Though this story serves as a prequel to Sleigh the Night: A Winter Shorts Collection, it can absolutely be read as a standalone as this is a complete (but short) story. The plot is simple:

Girl likes boy.

Boy likes girl.

Girl lets boy bend her over in the middle of a party.

That's it and that's all. If you're looking for something with a little more depth, this may not be for you. If this sounds like your jam, well then have fun.

TROPES

Brother's best friend, (not so) one night stand

TAGS

MF, low angst, standalone, prequel, summer fun, hand necklaces, black romance, plus-size FMC, "what's wrong with dry humping in the corner if no one's watching", "that time I let my brother's bestie smash in a house full of people", "jinkies, Velma gets freaky!"

CONTENT WARNINGS

This novella features content and themes throughout that may not be suitable for all readers. This includes, but is not limited to adult language, recreational alcohol consumption, explicit sexual content, and semi-public sex acts.

As with all Lady Marie projects, please read with care.

For the ones who will forever do it for the '99 and the 2000s

CHAPTER
ONE

| DEZIREÉ |

OKAY, *but I'm trying to be in my soft girl era too, Ari. Desperately.*

Hearing her sing about getting a chance to be soft felt like torture as I made my way toward the living room, eager to settle in for a night of sushi and wine. At the feel of my phone vibrating, I checked the screen.

My mama.

Maybe if I didn't answer, she'd give me a little bit of peace.

No such luck. As soon as a series of fresh vibrations started, I picked up knowing she would just keep calling if I didn't.

"Girl, I know your little behind wasn't sitting up there ignoring me."

"Of course not mama," I said, trying my hardest to sound offended. "And my behind is a lot of things, but little has never been one of them."

"You can thank your great-grandmother for that because my nana had hips and ass for days and she sure enough passed it down the line." She cackled at her own joke, and any other time, I would've been right there with her, but right now I just wanted peace and quiet.

"Anyway, do you still have those black pumps with the straps that tie all the way up your calf. The ones I picked up when we went to Gia's a few months ago."

"The heels with the gold butterflies?"

"Mhmm. You borrowed them three weeks ago and must've thought they were meant for you because I haven't seen them since."

"Mama, please," I snickered. "I just forgot is all."

"Sure you did with your lil' thieving ass. Well the point is I need them back. Your father is taking me dancing tomorrow." Just by her tone, it wasn't hard to guess she was smiling. She always did when she mentioned daddy, even when she tried to act like she couldn't stand the man.

"Yes, ma'am. I'll drop them by the house before I head to Kamille's tomorrow."

"Thank you, baby, but that won't be necessary. I already told your brother to stop by your place after his shift at the station."

I groaned, throwing my head back in irritation. "Ma, you know I hate when y'all just drop by without telling me." Damn, I was twenty-six. Couldn't I get some privacy.

"It's not a drop by if I'm calling, little girl."

Of course not. Just as I went to roll my eyes, she added, "And don't be over there rolling those beady eyes of yours either. You may be grown, but you're not too grown to get your behind tore up."

How in the... "Okay girl, no need for all that. I'll make sure the shoes are waiting by the front door."

"Thank you, baby. Now—" Before she could finish her thought, an announcement over the hospital intercom stopped her in her tracks. "Shoot. We'll have to talk later, Dezi, I've got to go. Oh! And give your brother your butterfly pendant too. It'll go perfectly with the shoes."

She ended the call, and as horrible as it sounded, I'd never been more grateful for a hospital emergency.

Now maybe I could start my favorite dating show. Since Ari had finished singing, I turned off the sound system ready to focus on the tv. And once again, I was interrupted by my phone ringing. That had to be the food.

"Kyle, if you're telling me you're downstairs already, I just might have to up your tip."

"Damn, shit getting so desperate you gotta pay for dick sis? Cold world."

I kissed my teeth, annoyance level skyrocketing immediately. I swear, no nigga could get on your nerves like one who slid out the womb before you. Eighteen months older than me and his ass still managed to be immature as hell.

"Shut up, Grayson. I thought you were my sushi delivery."

"Likely story, little sister. Likely story," he snickered.

"What do you want, Grayson? I'm busy." And my patience was in very short supply.

"Damn, that's how you treat your favorite brother these days? Wait 'til I tell your mama."

"Please! With your snitching ass."And you're my only brother, remember? Last time I checked, we have the same mama and non-rolling stone ass daddy too. Quite frankly, I'd return to sender if I could," I teased. "Now seriously, what do you want? I'm busy trying to decompress and you're fucking up my vibe."

"Must be nice to be able to kick your feet up. Some of us have been too busy running into burning buildings to do all that. I could be at home catching up on my sleep after working a straight twenty-four, but instead I'm checking on you." As if I needed another reminder about his all too important job as a firefighter.

"You ain't gotta lie, Craig," I laughed. "You're calling 'cause mommy told you to."

"Damn, that must be those top-notch lawyer deductive reasoning skills hard at work. I plead guilty, your honor!"

Despite myself, I was clutching my stomach, damn near in tears from laughing so hard. A whole clown.

"You caught me red-handed. I'll be pulling up in two minutes, so have them shoes ready 'cause I promise you, I'm not taking an ass-whooping from mama because you want to be on joke time."

Shit. Mama had literally just called. I thought I had at least an hour or two before he'd be on his way. Not bothering to point out the fact that he was the one joking around, I scrambled off the couch. "Right. Let me go dig those out of my closet."

"Make it quick 'cause I'm tired as shit. This is about to be an in-and-out mission and you know you move like Grandma Moses."

"Get off my line," I said, kissing my teeth before hanging up.

Since I'd skipped organizing my closet the last few weeks, finding the shoes took longer than I expected. By the time I managed to pull them out from under a few WNBA jerseys that I swear had been hanging up at some point, Grayson had already rung the doorbell twice. I'd just managed to snatch up the matching necklace when he went for lucky try number three.

"If your ashy ass rings my damn doorbell one more time…" I said, attitude ever present as I yanked the door open, ready to cuss him out. Only it wasn't his face smirking at me on the other side.

"My bad, Zee. Thought maybe you couldn't hear it or some shit."

That velvety baritone sent shots of electricity through my entire body. My teeth pulled at my bottom lip as I looked up into dark brown eyes that seemed to scan every inch of my body. Suddenly my gray off-the-shoulder t-shirt and black leggings didn't feel like enough clothing. Not when the look I was getting right now made me feel completely exposed.

"Hey, Izaiah." Shit. Why was it that every time I said this man's name, my voice sounded desperate? Needy…

*Maybe because you **need** him to put his hands on you...and a couple other things.*

Ignoring my own thoughts, I gave him a small smile. "Sorry, Zay. I thought you were a different, more annoying fire-fighter."

He chuckled and I swear my nipples pebbled almost instantly. How was that even a real thing? Swear I thought that was some shit authors just made up to sell books.

The joke was on me because by the way his eyes dipped down and looked directly at the traitorous ass demonstration, the shit was very real. Goddamn me and my refusal to wear a bra whenever I was at home. The fact that the only thing standing between us was a very thin shirt on my part made my cheeks heat.

"Damn, did you just call me annoying?" he joked.

Unintentionally. "Maybe. Gotta keep that ego in check so you stay humble."

Bitch, please, annoying is the last way you'd describe this nigga.

True, especially when there were so many other descriptors for the man standing in front of me.

Sexy.

Fine as hell.

The universe's gift to horny women everywhere.

My eyes swept over his body, taking in his dark chocolate skin that always looked good enough to eat, a neatly trimmed beard, tattoo-covered forearms that practically begged to be touched, and gray sweatpants that gave me a perfect visual of what he was hiding underneath.

Izaiah was a walking wet dream and I should know. I'd had plenty with him in the starring role.

When my eyes met his, it was obvious he'd caught me checking him out. Fuck it. He already knew how fine he was and it couldn't be the first time someone decided to appreciate the visual. Hell, it wasn't even the first time he'd probably caught me doing it.

From the moment my brother first introduced us, I'd been drawn to him. Between his looks, his laid-back mentality, and his all-around good guy persona, it was hard to pick just one reason. The way he tended to gravitate toward me told me that I wasn't alone.

And yet we were both apparently good with minimizing our dynamic to a bit of harmless teasing and flirting.

For now anyway.

But that didn't stop me from wondering what it would feel like to have his beard tickling my inner thighs as he—

"Zee, did you hear me?"

Hearing the nickname that only he used snapped me from my trance.

"Oh, umm…" I hadn't. "I might have missed that." No point in lying about what we both knew.

With a shake of his head, he repeated himself. "My truck is in the shop, so I'm catching a ride home with Gray. He asked me to come up and grab whatever you had for your mom. You got that for me?"

Oh, I got something for you if you really want it. That's for damn sure.

Instead of saying that aloud, what actually came out of my mouth was a simple "Mhmm!" as I held the bag in his direction.

Was it my imagination or did he purposely brush his fingers against mine? *Girl, get a grip and calm the hell down.*

"Bet," he said with a smile that made me want to drop my draws right then and there. I mean honestly, who needed pride when they could have a gorgeous, big dick nigga instead?

Fortunately—or maybe unfortunately—I didn't have time to offer myself up on a silver platter since the usual delivery guy from my preferred sushi spot was rounding the corner.

"Hey Kyle. Let me run and grab my wallet," I said, looking for any excuse to get my shit together, but Izaiah shook his head.

"Nah, I got it." He didn't even give me a chance to protest. Just immediately grabbed his wallet from his pocket, counted off way too much money, and slipped it into the boy's hands.

"You didn't have to do that," I said as soon as Kyle disappeared.

"Maybe not, but I did it anyway."

"Oh, I'm not complaining. More like an observation." One protest was all he'd get from me and it was barely that. "I'll be sure to return the favor. Maybe."

"Noted."

We stood there for a few more moments just staring at one another, wondering who would make the next move. Was there even a next move to make?

Finally, the corner of his lips turned up in a smile. "I'll catch you later, Zee," he said, backing away.

"Oh I'm sure you will. Just remember that offer has an expiration date." I asked, giving him a smile of my own.

"Mmmm." His tongue ran over his bottom lip, the heat in his eyes obvious despite the small distance he'd created between us. "I'm not too worried about it. If you're eager to offer up something, though…I'll be sure to keep that in mind."

By the time I managed to close the door, my entire body felt like it was on fire. The type only one fireman in particular would be able to put out.

Fuck sushi.

Right now, dessert was calling my name, and I knew just which toy and fantasy I was going to use to answer.

CHAPTER
TWO

| IZAIAH |

"DAMN, bruh. I sent your ass up there thinking it'd speed up the process, not take twice as long."

I barely had one foot in the truck and Grayson was already complaining. It wasn't fazing me, but damn, his ass was predictable as fuck.

"Chill. I had to wait for her to answer the door. It didn't even take that long for real."

And when she did finally answer, the last thing I was thinking about was grabbing a pair of shoes.

As soon as I saw Dezireé, the only thing on my mind was grabbing her fine ass and taking her back inside. How else were we going to get back to her room so I could find out how she tasted? And unless I was trippin', the hungry look she'd been giving me suggested she wanted the same thing. Maybe that was just wishful thinking on my part. Or maybe I was a little delusional. Who the fuck knew?

Every time I was in her presence, it got harder to resist her beautiful ass. I tried to keep shit low-key out of respect for both her and her brother, but I'd be a bold-faced liar if I said I didn't want to wrap those thick thighs around my shoulders and eat her from top to bottom and front to back.

Deziree, or Zee as I called her, had held the starring role in each and every one of my dreams for a very long time. Her amber brown skin, naturally long lashes, and thick plus-size frame drew me in from the very start. And that smile? It was hard not to be mesmerized by it. Even in the pictures I'd seen of her wearing braces, it'd been gorgeous enough to stop traffic.

And while a lesser nigga might've been turned off by her attitude, it only made me want to be around her that much more. Baby girl had both bark and bite and I loved that shit. It turned me on knowing that she didn't back down from me, or anyone else for that matter. A mouth like hers was my weakness.

Zee's confidence and attitude were two of the sexiest things about her.

"Whatever, nigga. Y'all probably got lost in each other's eyes or some shit. That's my bad for real 'cause I really shouldn't have sent your ass up there in the first place. Neither one of y'all can focus when the other is around."

Okay, so obviously the fact that I was feeling my best friend's sister hadn't gone unnoticed. Guess subtlety wasn't my strong suit.

If the way I couldn't take my eyes off of her when we first met hadn't clued him in, the fact that I spent the next week adding her name to random conversations every time we were on shift together did. Instead of wanting to beat my ass like another nigga might have, he just laughed and gave me shit about it every chance he could.

Like right now.

"Man, it wasn't even like that. I just wasn't trying to rush her to keep your impatient ass happy." *Lying ass.* "By the time she came to the door, a delivery showed up and we just got distracted while she sorted that out."

Gray shook his head. "Be fucking for real, Zay. I'm smarter than a fifth grader."

"Not by much," I snickered.

"Fuck you." He kissed his teeth as he pulled up to a red light, taking his eyes off the road to turn them on me. "I wish your ass would just ask her out already. All this lovesick puppy shit is tired as fuck. I can't be walking around with a pathetic ass nigga, in or outside of the firehouse. What are you even waiting for? Her and that nigga Matthew ain't been together for like a year."

Trust me, I know.

Had I been keeping track since they broke up?

Maybe.

"I keep telling you I'm not on that type of time. Don't act like her and that nigga weren't together for years. Like on some college sweethearts shit. Ain't that what you told me? That ain't something you just get over immediately."

"It is when it didn't make any sense in the first place. I mean, he's cool people and I fuck with him and all, but that shit was never meant to last beyond the first year. I don't care what anybody says."

"And yet it did."

Grayson only shrugged as he pulled off again, heading in the direction of my place.

"I'm not trying to pressure her into some shit she's not ready for. We're friends. That's it, that's all, and we're both good with that."

"Yeah, okay. Y'all might be fooling each other, but I promise you, it's not working on anybody else."

He let silence take over for a few minutes, leaving me to my thoughts before he spoke again. "And I can't believe you're still out here calling her Zee when you know her name now, nigga. And she just be letting you get away with that shit."

I chuckled remembering it like it happened yesterday. When Gray first told me about his sister, he called her Dee. Unfortunately, because he always said it in such a rush, what I'd heard was *Zee*. When we finally met and I called her what I thought was her nickname, she burst out laughing before responding, *"Who?"*

I didn't understand what the problem was until I repeated myself and heard her say, *"This nigga..."* under her breath. After rolling her eyes and making a point to show me how annoyed she was, she corrected me.

"My name is Dezireé, sir. D-E-Z-I-R-E-É. Dee, Dezi, or

Dezireé. Those are all very acceptable versions of my name, but I don't know shit about a bitch named Zee."

I could've been embarrassed, but I was so mesmerized by the way she called herself putting me in my place, I decided to play that shit off instead.

"I know what your name is, but since I'm finna be a special person in your life, shouldn't I get to call you by a special name too? Be all memorable and shit."

In reality, I would've agreed to call her whatever she wanted me to, especially if it meant I got to call her mine.

Luckily for me, instead of going off, she just kissed her teeth, gave me that cute little half-smile of hers, and walked away. Nickname officially solidified, never to be challenged again.

"What can I say? I guess I'm just that nigga for real. Don't be mad 'cause she likes me more than you," I said, coming back to the present.

"We already covered this. You're a scared ass nigga, not a real one." He chuckled as he made the turn onto my street. "And if she liked me how she likes you, that'd be some sick shit. It's laws against that type of thing. No, thanks."

"And see, that's exactly why people are always ready to cuss your ass out," I groaned. "That's the real difference between the two of us. You're irritating and I'm Prince Charming. The facts are just the facts."

"Mmhmm, and the facts say you're scary as fuck. Actually, it's probably a good thing you're not trying to ask her out. Last thing I need is for my sister to be dating a nigga who probably couldn't even square up and handle business if someone ran up on her."

"Fuck you."

"Thanks, but nah."

I reached over and shoved him, but he wasn't fazed in the least. Grayson lived to torment my ass. Shit, he lived to torment everybody, now that I thought about it.

"Didn't anyone ever teach you not to put your hands on the driver? You're lucky we're here or I'd make your ass walk home."

Yeah, right. There was no way he would have put me out of his truck and we both knew it.

"Anyway, you figure out if you coming through tomorrow?"

I didn't have the slightest idea what he was talking about. My ass was exhausted as fuck and now that we were in my driveway, all I could think about was washing this shift off of me and letting my head hit the pillow. "Coming through for..."

"*Kamille's Birthday Extravaganza* or whatever the fuck she's calling it these days."

Shit, I'd forgotten all about that.

"Come on, Zay, you ain't about to have me catching all the ass at this party by myself, are you?"

"All what ass 'cause you know damn well Kamille ain't throwing you none." Now it was my turn to laugh.

He scowled. "Ain't nobody thinking about that damn woman."

"Yeah, a'ight." Whether he admitted it or not, his little sister's best friend got under his skin in more ways than one. I'd never really gotten the history there, but anyone who spent more than ten minutes with them could see the chemistry. Whether or not it was romantic or something that would lead to an ass-whooping was still up for debate.

"Don't deflect. You coming or not?"

Right, the birthday party, which for some reason was a costume party in the middle of May. I usually had to miss it, but for once, I was actually free. And any opportunity to see Dezireé was one I was going to take.

"You asking about me, but didn't you tell me you got permanently banned from her house during last year's party? How you finna make it through the door?"

All I knew was that something happened that neither of them would give details on, and whatever it was ended with Kamille dumping a bowl of rum punch all over him and threatening to drag him out the house by his locs.

Gray shrugged. "That was just a misunderstanding. As long as I stay out of her way, Kamille won't care whether I'm there or not. Too much other shit will be going on."

"You mean as long as you bob and weave, duck and hide, she shouldn't notice that you crashed her party and toss you out on your ass."

"Same thing."

Grayson was wild, but he was my boy. From the moment I'd started at the station, we'd connected. I'd dropped the majority of my friends before moving to Oakwood and starting over. Sure, I'd met some people, but it wasn't until Grayson sat his ass across from me at the station that I found an actual friend. Someone to call my brother. So even though getting a chance to see Deziree two days in a row definitely had its merits, I also wasn't about to let my boy face the birthday girl on his own.

"Actually, you know what? Yeah, I think I will slide through."

Grayson gave me a knowing look.

"I bet." He smirked before adding, "Now get the fuck out so I can go see my mama."

CHAPTER
THREE

| DEZIREÉ |

HALLOWEEN WAS one of my favorite times of year and had been ever since my trick-or-treating days, so when Kamille announced that she wanted to have a costume party for her big two-six, it didn't matter to me that the holiday was technically five months away. Was there a rule that said you could only wear costumes once a year? Hell no.

And if there was… Well, rules were meant to be broken.

Checking myself out in the mirror, my lips turned up in a smirk.

Girl, you look the fuck good.

Orange fishnet tights with a matching halter top perfectly zig-zagged up my legs well past where the short red pleated skirt ended, showing off my thick thighs. My wide hips and round ass looked *phenomenal*. I'd been skeptical about wearing a wig, especially since it was a short bob with bangs, but it set off the entire look, especially once I slid on a pair of lensless glasses. I did miss my usual 4C twist out, but I'd survive for the night.

Velma Dinkley wished she looked this good.

"Bitch, do you know what I did with my go-go boots?"

Kamille's loud ass was going to get a noise complaint before the night was out. "They're in the second guestroom. That's where you tried them on the other day for me and Trina, right?"

At the mention of her name, the third member of our trio walked by, work phone in hand. I narrowed my eyes. That was supposed to be stashed away somewhere—preferably at home—but I'd let it slide for now.

The three of us had been thick as thieves since we were in diapers. Okay, so that was a bit of an exaggeration. Kamille and I had been attached at the hip since we were six, and when Trina moved to town in fifth grade, well, she just fit perfectly.

And tonight, in honor of our iconic friendship, we'd decided to pay homage to three members of Mystery Inc.

"Ewww, you lil' nasty," Kamille said, nose scrunched as I met her in the hallway just as Trina disappeared. "Where are your clothes? Who raised you?"

Laughing, I flipped her off. "Miss ma'am, we have on the same amount of clothing, so if I'm nasty, so are you." My very fine friend had opted for an all-lace lavender slip dress that clung to her slim frame as though it'd been painted on for her interpretation of Daphne Blake. "Really, I might have on more. I swear if you bend over even an inch tonight, the people are going to see your uterus."

"Oh, girl, kiss my ass 'cause with all that junk in your trunk? Baby, they'll be paying for tickets to your show long before they see mine."

"Aww, don't count yourself out, boo. Little booties matter too."

"You tried it," she said, smacking her lips.

I blew her a kiss as she walked back into her room to put the finishing touches on her outfit. Kamille was even more of a mess than I was sometimes, but that's why I loved her.

Following right behind her, I leaned against the door frame. "We're about to have a fucking time, okay! I don't think the people are ready, but they better fall in line." I paused. "Have I told you happy birthday yet?"

"Only about twenty times since midnight," she giggled. "But I love hearing it, so keep it coming."

"Well, then happy birthday, bitch!" screamed Trina as she made her way into the room, work phone nowhere in sight. She even gave us a little preview as she bent over and twerked in her open long-sleeved white button-up tie shirt, electric blue leather hot pants, ascot, and some cute ass sneakers that I prayed to God no one stepped on. Fucking up her shoes was the quickest way to have Trina on your ass.

"How much longer do we have before people get here?"

Kamille fluffed her light brown coils. "Not long." I swear her hair got bigger every time I saw her, which was a whole hell of a lot. After another second, she turned to me with a concerned look. "Are you sure it's okay I invited Matthew?"

Not this again. I didn't even need to look at Trina for fear she was wearing the same expression, especially since she'd been seeing Matt a lot more lately since his job had him flying in and out of New York, where she lived. Ever since we'd broken up, it was like everyone was walking on eggshells when it came to the two of us. When my parents weren't pushing for us to get back together, my friends were acting like I was going to have a breakdown if he happened to be in the same room.

I'd broken up with him, but somehow I was supposed to be the fragile one. That was wild because Deziree Jackson and *fragile* didn't even belong in the same sentence.

Date a nigga for five years and suddenly you're supposed to either be *with* him forever or be hung up *on* him forever.

Well, I was neither. As much as I loved Matt, ours was not a forever type of thing. I wanted—*needed*—something different. I appreciated my girls trying to look out for me, but I'd appreciate it more if they just gave it a rest. At least for tonight.

"Kami, don't ask me that again. I told you it's fine. We're all friends and have been long before the two of us ever started dating. Things don't need to change just because we aren't together anymore." I looked at both of them. "We're good."

Honestly, this was probably my fault. If I'd never crossed that line with Matt during our last year of college, this wouldn't even be an issue. Dating him was just supposed to be something fun, and it was. We were attracted to one another, had the same career goals, the sex was bomb, and we'd started off as friends first, so what was the harm?

Apparently more than I'd realized because before long, everyone around us was planning a future that we had no say in. We loved each other, there was no doubt in my mind about that, but we weren't in love and to me there was a big difference.

So, when it was clear the romantic side of things had run its course for us, I was more than happy to say the quiet part out loud. His job offer in San Francisco made it that much easier. A weight was lifted off both our shoulders the day I told him a long-distance relationship wasn't right for either of us and that it was time we went our separate ways. Maybe no one else understood, but they didn't need to.

"Okay, okay, I just had to check one more time." Kamille pulled me into a hug.

Trina jumped in quickly. "And check you have, so our bestie duties are officially fulfilled."

I shot her an appreciative look. Since she was the one to end the conversation, maybe Kamille would actually listen and let it go.

"Besides, the only person Dezi really needs to be avoiding tonight is her brother. He's going to have a fit when he sees that outfit," she added with a snicker.

"Oh, he won't have time to be worried about her because he'll be too focused on dodging my fists if that nigga actually shows his ugly ass face in my house." I've never seen Kamille move as fast as she did, stomping into the bathroom.

Trina and I shot each other a look. We didn't know what the hell had happened last year to tip Kami over the edge, but ever since, Grayson had gone from my annoying older brother to public enemy number one. If he wanted to keep his face—and his balls—intact, he should probably stay his ass home.

But that would mean no chance of seeing Izaiah tonight either.

And what a true tragedy that would be.

"I'm serious Dez, he steps one foot into this house and I'm stomping him out with these boots. And Trina is going to help me."

"Uh, hell no I'm not," Trina said as she pulled apart a few of her curled burgundy-tipped locs. "I'm not getting blood all over my new Indigo Girl A'Ones just 'cause a nigga wants to try his luck. Do you know what I had to do to get these? Baby cakes, you finna be on your own with that one."

"Wooow. You know what? That's fine. I'm more than capable of handling him myself anyway."

On second thought, I wasn't sure if seeing Izaiah was worth the price of having to help my mama plan Grayson's funeral.

"Alright, Rocky Balboa, calm down. And hurry your ass up. We're ready to drink." I went to grab my red furry slippers 'cause real shoes were not in my plans tonight and met Trina in the hallway, looping my arm with hers.

With the furniture rearranged to give everyone plenty of space to dance, a full bar, and food set up in the kitchen, the house was more than ready for guests. The cauldrons, cobwebs, skeletons and other spooky decor set the mood perfectly. My girl really went all out this year.

"Ladies, I'd like to raise a toast." Kamille appeared at the bar, putting shots in all of our hands. "To the ass we're about to throw and the niggas who just might get to catch it!"

That, of course, earned shrieks and laughter from both me and Trina.

"And to the birthday girl! May twenty-six treat you like the bad bitch you are. Or at least a whole lot better than those bad ass kids you work with," I giggled before throwing back my shot of whiskey.

"Amen to that!" they said as they followed suit.

Let the festivities begin.

CHAPTER
FOUR

| DEZIREÉ |

BLESS TRINA, but the mini crab cake tray she'd stolen from the food table wasn't doing a damn thing to soak up the three shots of cognac or the mixed drink I'd had in the two hours since the party had started. I needed to get my hands on a bottle of water and something a little more substantial.

No one seemed to be paying me any mind as I weaved my way through the crowd. They were too busy dancing, drinking, or playing something that looked—and smelled—suspiciously like tequila pong. Then, of course, there was the game of strip spades going on in the corner. Yeah…niggas were definitely in here wildin', but that wasn't necessarily a bad thing.

"Deziiiii!" shouted a voice above the noise, stopping me in my tracks.

Kamille landed in front of me, throwing her little ass to the beat of the Flo Milli song coming through the speakers.

"Ayyyye!" I screamed, hyping my girl up.

"Girl, I think this might be my best party yet." Kamille threw back a shot I hadn't even noticed and set the empty glass down on one of the high tables.

"You might be right." With a sigh, I added, "You have no idea how much I needed this." The stress of work had been so much lately that I'd decided to take a sabbatical. Things were tough and not everyone knew about it, but I was hoping the time away from the office would give me the relief I needed.

Before she could ask for details, a Megan Thee Stallion song came through the speakers providing the perfect distraction.

I let the words flow through me so naturally that you would've thought I'd written them myself. A small crowd formed and off their energy alone, I put my all into the performance, with Trina coming out of nowhere to back me up.

Dropping down, I showed off the Megan knees I had to match my rapping skills, only to be interrupted by the most irritating ass voice imaginable.

"What the fuck do you have on, bruh?"

One look from Trina confirmed what I already knew. My brother had indeed decided to crash the party.

I kissed my teeth standing and turning to face Grayson. "Here you go. I swear you be having the worst fucking timing."

Why was it that every time a bad bitch was in the middle of giving the performance of her life, a nigga just had to show up and ruin shit?

Recognizing that this show was over, the crowd slowly went about their business. Of course, because he was so damn dramatic, he was staring at me like I had two heads and one of them had just smacked our mama.

Showing his ass over my costume when he hadn't even bothered to wear one was wild work. The best he could do was his actual fire department t-shirt and work pants? Really?

No vision.

"A costume, obviously."

"I know you fuckin' lying. What makes you think I want to see your ass hanging out all damn night?"

I couldn't help but snicker. "That sounds like a *you* problem, Gracie." He hated the nickname I'd given him when we were kids, which only made me want to use it more. "Especially since you're not even supposed to be here."

My gaze was drawn to a figure behind him and I couldn't help but smirk. "What about you, Izaiah? Do you like my costume?"

To emphasize my question, I did a little spin. There was no missing the way his eyes traced over me from top to bottom, waking the butterflies in my stomach.

"It's definitely something." He took a step forward and licked his lips. What would it feel like to have them wrapped around my—

"Fuck both of y'all. Just fuckin' nasty," Grayson interrupted. "And you, Dee, are just a straight asshole 'cause you know that's my favorite cartoon. How am I supposed to watch Scooby and the gang now?

I shrugged. "Again, not my problem."

"You cold-blooded. For real," he groaned.

"And you're pushing your luck. Shouldn't you be hiding so Kami doesn't catch you in here?" My eyes searched the room looking for Kamille, who had disappeared during my little performance with Trina. "Matter of fact, you might wanna do a little less talking and a little more blending in before someone gives her a heads up."

I moved in closer and patted his cheek. "And by someone, I mean me."

"You'd really snitch on your own blood like that?"

He tried hitting me with the puppy dog eyes, but he should've known better. "If it'd get you up out my face? Absolutely."

"Looks like someone beat you to it," Trina said, causing all of our eyes to lock in on Kamille headed toward us. "Cheer up, Grayson! I mean honestly, Velma was always out of your league anyway."

"Scooby's out of his fucking league," Kamille added as she stopped in front of us. My girl really didn't miss a beat with that one.

"Good thing I'd rather try my hand at Daphne," he shot back. "From what I heard, she's right on my level."

Awww shit. Okay, it was time to break these two up before shit got ugly. Thankfully, I wasn't the only one who saw trouble brewing.

"A'ight, chill. Everyone back to your corners." Izaiah stepped in front of Grayson and whispered something the rest of us couldn't hear. Whatever he said worked because after one more quick glance, Grayson did himself a favor and walked off without another word.

"Yeah, scurry along, please. Have a drink. Grab some food. Get a life!" Kamille called after him.

I said a silent thank you as she went in the opposite direction. Babysitting either one of them was not on my agenda for the night. Trina gave me a look of her own before heading after Kamille, probably to check on her. Good. I swear, if my knucklehead ass brother ruined tonight for her, he wouldn't have to worry about Kami beating his ass because I'd do it for her.

The feel of someone's hand wrapping around my own pulled my attention.

"You good?"

There was no stopping the warm feeling that spread through me at the concern in Zay's voice.

"Always." I cocked my head to the side as I looked up at him. "Not you popping up on me tonight."

"What you mean?" he asked, brows knitted in confusion.

"You never come to Kamille's birthday. Always too busy, right?" My tone was teasing and I was glad when a smile spread across his face in response.

"Why you tryna play me like that, Zee?"

"Like what?"

"Like I wouldn't be ready to come running any time you called."

Was this nigga *trying* to ruin my draws? If so, mission accomplished. Between the low, husky tone of his words, the way his eyes seemed to see right through me, and how that tongue of his swept over his plump lips, I just knew my pussy was soaked.

"Now how would I know that if I've never tested the theory?" Even with the little bit of attitude behind my words, I still managed to sound breathless.

"Maybe you should."

I usually wouldn't be able to resist a challenge, but a girl should at least try and fake a little self-restraint, right?

For what? Girl, stop playing and let that man bend you over!

Shit, if he keeps testing me, I just might.

Ignoring the little devil on my shoulder, I cleared my throat and gave him a once-over.

"Now correct me if I'm wrong, but isn't Clark Kent the one who wears the glasses?" I asked, gesturing to the combination of his Superman t-shirt and lensless glasses. "Seems to me you're breaking some sort of comic book rule advertising your alter ego like this."

"True, but if you're gonna dock points for that, then I get to do the same 'cause I damn sure don't remember Velma filling out her skirt the way you are right now."

He reached out and fingered the edge of the skirt in question and it took everything in me not to whimper when the action made my pussy clench.

"Well, I guess we're both just doing whatever the fuck we want tonight then, huh?"

If only.

"Guess so."

His scent was so intoxicating that I had to press my thighs together to try and relieve the pressure I was feeling. Why did he have to smell so goddamn good? What did he do, go to the fine nigga store and tell them to spray him with whatever fragrance would have women ready to fuck him on sight?

"I'm finna go ahead and give you your space."

"Gotta make sure that brother of mine doesn't get yanked the fuck up?"

"Something like that," he chuckled. "But let me say, for the record, I'm looking forward to the next show you put on." He backed away. "And I'm around if you decide you need a co-star."

Damn. Damn. Damn. "I'll try and remember that. If you think you can keep up, I mean."

"You ain't said nothing but a word."

My eyes tracked him as he moved through the crowd.

I swear he had no right to be that fucking fine. By the way half the women in the room also couldn't take their eyes off him, I wasn't the only one who noticed. Actually, there were way too many of these bitches looking at him if you asked me. They ain't have shit else to do? I mean damn, he ain't the only cute man up in here.

Bitch, it's not like you have a claim on his ass.

Not yet anyway.

And could I really blame them for staring? Izaiah made Superman look too fucking good, even if it wasn't a full costume. It was probably for the best that he'd chosen to skip the spandex 'cause ain't no way I was going to be able to keep my hands to myself if he'd showed up in tights, full package on display.

Just as the thought crossed my mind, one of the teachers from Kamille's job stopped Izaiah, pulling him into a hug.

Now how the fuck does he know her? I asked myself as something that felt suspiciously like jealousy tugged at my gut. It only grew when she threw her head back, laughing as her fingers grazed his arm.

He ain't that damn funny, girl.

I was so caught up watching them, I didn't even notice when a familiar figure walked up next to me.

"You stare any harder, Dezi, and you're gonna burn a hole in both their heads."

I'd know that voice anywhere.

Sure enough, I turned to find Matthew and his signature sheepish smile staring down at me. I nudged him with my shoulder. "Not you calling me out. You can't ever let me live, can you?"

"I like to think I'm just keeping you honest. Always have, always will."

A smile spread across my lips at his words. Thank god we'd moved beyond the awkward break-up stage, despite what everyone else seemed to think. Now we were just the same friends we'd been since the moment we met. Well, except for the fact that he'd seen me naked and I knew what his dick felt like, but that was beside the point. If nothing else, we were in a place where neither one of us had to feel weird about the way he'd caught me staring at another man or even talking about it.

"Whatever. What do you want, *Kid*?" I asked, referencing the fact that he was dressed as the lead character from his favorite movie.

"Damn, a nigga gotta want something? Maybe I just came over to say hi to the bestie who's been ducking and dodging me since I got to town last week."

"Boy, ain't nobody been dodging your ass. I've just been busy."

"Yeah, okay, tell me anything. Acting like as soon as I see you, I'm gonna drop my draws or something."

"Oh my god!" I screamed, drawing attention to us. I gave him a playful shove before pulling him into a hug. "Shut the hell up. See, this is why I can't stand your ass."

"And yet here you are, all hugged up on me."

I giggled as he tightened his grip. "I'm just trying to help your ole ungrateful ass out. If I don't give you a lil' play, who will?" I teased.

Was it my imagination or did he stiffen for just a second?

"You'd be surprised," he said, and I pulled back because there was something in his voice I couldn't quite figure out.

Whatever it was disappeared with a quickness. The only thing there now was that same cute ass smile that always seemed to work in his favor. It was those damn dimples of his. They literally made old ladies swoon whenever he offered to help them cross the street.

"Something's up with you." My eyes narrowed with suspicion as he feigned innocence. "But luckily for you, I had just enough to drink to not push it right now."

I broke our hug but held onto his hand as I led him toward the den. "Come on, *friend*. Let's see if we can convince the DJ to play 'Ain't My Type of Hype' just for you."

"Ughhh," he groaned. "Do we have to?"

"You brought it on yourself coming here dressed like that. Might as well suck it up 'cause you're going to give me what I want."

"And what's that?"

"A dance, duh."

It didn't matter that we both knew how much he hated dancing. He was going to do it anyway because that's just the type of guy Matthew was. Whatever woman ended up with him in the end was going to be one lucky girl.

CHAPTER
FIVE

| IZAIAH |

"I'VE GOT to hand it to Kamille. She definitely knows how to throw a party."

An absentminded nod was all I could manage since I was barely paying attention to Gray. Something more important had my focus.

Like the fact that for the last hour, Deziree and her ex had been attached at the goddamn hip. What the fuck was that about?

Logically, I knew I had no right to be jealous, but it was taking everything in me not to react every time she bent over in that pleated skirt and gave him and every other nigga in this motherfucka a peek at her perfect ass.

It shouldn't bother me. I knew that, and yet I wanted to go over there and knock that nigga clear across the room for having the audacity to be that close to her. Even now, when the only thing they seemed to be doing was sharing a plate of food, my hand kept flexing like I was itching to hit somebody.

Deziree was like the last drink of water and I was the thirstiest nigga in the room.

The sudden closeness of Gray snapping his fingers in front of my face broke the spell she had me under. "You not even listening to me, nigga."

"Yes, I am." And even though I tried to say it as convincingly as possible, we both knew it was a lie.

"Oh, yeah? What I just say?"

"A bunch of bullshit when what you should've been saying is how glad you are Kamille ain't whoop your ass for crashing her party."

He kissed his teeth. "Haha, very funny. Goofy ass. Ain't nobody worried about Kamille. There's entirely too many fine women in here for me to be caught up in her the way you're caught up over my sister's ass." He balled up his face in disgust. "At least wipe the drool of your chin, nigga, damn."

All he did was laugh as I flipped him off. Or maybe he was laughing because I was trying—and failing—to discreetly check if I really was drooling.

Just then, a particularly thick version of a certain blonde dragon queen made her way into the kitchen, catching Grayson's attention.

"While you sit here and lie to yourself, I'm finna go handle some business. I suddenly got a craving for somebody sweet."

I chuckled, taking another sip of my drink as he left me to my own thoughts. As pathetic as it might have been, it took less than sixty seconds for my eyes to find Deziree again. This time I'd caught her as she threw her head back to laugh at something her ex was whispering in her ear.

Like that nigga is really that funny.

Why was it getting harder and harder to stick to what I'd told Grayson just twenty-four hours ago about not wanting to be on that type of time with her right now? The liquor in my system definitely wasn't helping.

Neither was the way her hips moved as a new song began to play through the speakers. I couldn't even tell you which one because I was too enthralled with the way she was vibing, hips whining, eyes closed like there was no one else in the room.

Her body was calling out for me. Or maybe I was imagining that shit. It didn't matter because whichever way I tried to tell the story, the result was the same. The perfect excuse for why I was allowing my feet to lead me out of the kitchen and straight to the woman I just couldn't seem to stay away from. And maybe this was where the universe wanted me to be since Matthew had suddenly disappeared leaving her on her own.

"I see you're back to putting on a show," I whispered in her ear as my arm wrapped around her waist and her body landed flush against mine.

She tensed for a split second before relaxing in my hold.

"Baby, I never stopped. Don't act like you didn't already know."

"And how would I know that?"

"You've been staring at me for the last thirty minutes, Zay. Probably longer, but I won't put your business out there too bad. I might be a little concerned if you weren't so damn cute."

She giggled, her arm reaching up to wrap around the back of my neck as she began to move again. I didn't say anything, too focused on the feel of her.

"Cat got your tongue? Don't tell me I make you nervous."

The taunts slipping from her lips shouldn't turn me on, but they did, just like everything else about her.

"Now you should know better than that, Zee." My fingertips grazed a bit of exposed skin. There was no mistaking the gasp she made as I stroked her thigh, the openings in her tights giving me the perfect amount of access.

"I'm just saying," she said as the whine of her hips began to slow and become more concentrated, forcing me to follow her lead. "Had me worried for a minute that you'd forgotten about me. Too busy being teacher's pet and whatnot earlier."

It took a second to understand what she was talking about, but once it hit me, I smirked. *Yvonne.* "No need to be jealous, Zee. I promise you, she's not who I want."

I meant it too. Yvonne had called herself flirting with me ever since I'd spoken to her fourth graders during Career Day a few months back. Honestly, I was only there as a favor to

Grayson after he'd flaked on Kamille. No matter how much she gave me the green light, though, I had no interest in taking her up on the offer.

"Yeah, okay. Tell me anything. So what kept you away? I know you're not scared of Grayson's ass."

"Never that."

And I meant it too, though part of me did wonder how serious he was about being okay with me hollering at Zee. Was he just talking shit because he thought I wouldn't follow through? I might be his boy, but at the end of the day, Gray was just as protective as any other big brother. Disrespecting Deziree wasn't something he'd tolerate, and while that was something I'd never do, it didn't mean some of the shit I'd been thinking about doing *to* and *with* her might not appear on his list of what he considered disrespectful.

"If that's the story you want to go with," she laughed. "So you just kept me waiting for the hell of it?" She turned her head enough to look me dead in the eye. "Cause silly me, I didn't think you were such a tease." There was a mischievous glint in her eyes. One that had me wondering what exactly I'd gotten myself into. "I thought that was my job."

Taking the lead, Deziree led us from the middle of the dance floor to an unoccupied corner, giving us a lot more privacy.

"You know you talking all that shit, but you could've easily come and found me yourself. Then again, you did seem to be occupied by your lil' friend."

Deziree turned so she was facing me, a confused look on her face. "Lil' friend?"

I nodded. "Looked like a whole ass reunion to me."

Gripping my shirt, Deziree pulled me in until I was crowding her space. We'd only been dancing for a minute, if that, but I already missed how perfectly her body fit against mine. The way her ass had pressed against my dick should've been a crime, but it was one I was more than happy to get locked up over. Fuck freedom. The woman in front of me was so much sweeter.

"Now who's jealous, Zay?"

Was I supposed to deny it?

"And what if I was?"

Damn, nigga. Not a lick of shame, huh?

"Well, I guess if it got you off your ass, a little jealousy might not be so bad."

She was right; it wasn't. Not when that was the reason my hands had the opportunity to slowly make their way up her skirt.

Was my dick bricking up simply because I was touching her or did it have more to do with her leading my hand to her barely covered ass? Either way, I felt like I was going to bust through my goddamn jeans. Denying the effect she was having on me was a lost fucking cause.

Goddamn.

Her hips began to move, grinding against me in time with the music. The way baby girl circled her hips had me wishing we didn't have so many clothes between us.

You know what? Fuck all that other shit I'd been talking about before. Whoever that nigga was, he was talking out his ass because there was nothing I wanted more than Dezireé. Maybe it was the music or maybe it was the liquor. Shit, maybe it was the whole vibe of the night. I didn't know, but right here, right now in this corner, I was sick of fucking pretending that this thing between us wasn't the most real shit I'd ever felt. The only shit that mattered.

Zee wrapped one leg around my waist, opening herself up to me and giving me the space I needed to press in between her thighs. It was the perfect position to wedge myself right up against her center.

"*Izaiah.*"

Now how the fuck was I supposed to live without hearing her moan my name like that again?

I leaned my forehead against hers, trying and failing to ground myself. Using the friction of my jeans because *goddamn,* they had to be good for something, I thrust against her and was rewarded with a whimper.

"What if I said I want you so bad right now, I can taste it?" My words ghosted across the space just below her ear.

Yeah, the Hennessy was definitely hitting right now, but I knew that even without it, I'd be intoxicated by her presence alone. I let my lips move over her skin until I found a spot on her neck that had her making that sound again. This time when I heard it, what little control I'd been holding onto snapped.

Nigga, what control? That shit left the building ten minutes ago.

Trusting that she'd keep her leg right where it was, I moved my hand away from her thigh and down between us instead.

"What would I find if I touched you right now, baby girl? Are you wet for me?"

I pulled back just in time to see the challenge in her eyes. "Why don't you tell me?"

Keeping my gaze locked on hers, I traced my fingers across her barely covered lips, this time letting the groan I'd held back earlier break through as I found the answer to my question.

Wet wasn't even the word. She was practically dripping.

"Feels like a yes to me." I paused. "But I want to hear you say it."

Nah, it was *necessary* for me to hear her say it.

Deziree moved one of her hands until it gripped my dick, and even with my jeans between us, I still couldn't help it when "*fuck*" slipped from my lips. "If this is going to be my prize for winning, then I'd say it's actually a hell yes."

Her words propelled us, our lips crashed together, ready to devour each other in whatever way we could. The taste of bourbon and caramel hit my tongue, causing me to moan.

That shit just might be my new favorite flavor.

Our tongues tangled, fighting for dominance and desperate for another taste. Somehow, it still wasn't enough.

Fuck dancing. That shit was an afterthought now. All I wanted was to get her somewhere that would allow me to feel her full warmth wrapped around my fingers without the possibility of someone else seeing.

Dezireé pulled away, a hushed *"Come on!"* leaving her as she stood, moving my fingers from under her skirt and grabbing my hand to lead me toward a closed door just a few steps away.

It didn't even occur to me that we probably had no business going wherever she was leading me. Why would it when the woman of my fucking dreams was reading my mind? If that meant we were asking for trouble, well shit…so be it.

Maybe trouble was exactly what I needed to get into tonight.

CHAPTER
SIX

| DEZIREÉ |

SOMETIMES, a woman should exercise a little self-control.

Okay, but is the self-control in the room with us?

Apparently not, considering all it took was half a dance before I found myself leading a nigga down to my friend's basement to have my way with him.

This wasn't just any nigga, though. It was Zay. Izaiah.

And as far as I was concerned, this was a long time coming.

So yeah, actually, self-control was overrated.

The quiet of the basement increased the intensity of the moment. Was this supposed to feel awkward? Because it didn't.

Was I supposed to be embarrassed by how forward I'd been? Because trust me, I wasn't.

The only thing I was actually feeling was need. As in I *needed* to know what it was like to come all over his dick. You would've thought finally getting to kiss him would have left me somewhat satisfied, but it had the opposite effect. Now I just wanted more.

As we reached the bottom of the stairs, Izaiah leaned in again, his tongue sliding along the seam of my lips as if he was begging to be let in. He didn't have to ask twice. I was ready to give this man whatever he wanted. If kissing him could soak the seat of my panties like this, I could only imagine what it would be like to have his tongue in other places.

"You are so fucking sexy," Izaiah whispered against my lips.

I smirked as I backed away, crooking my finger for him to follow. "Flattery will get you everywhere."

I didn't stop until the washing machine pressed against the back of my thighs and his body was crowding mine the same way it'd been upstairs. There was nowhere to run or hide.

Good.

"This," he said, fingering the edges of my wig, "needs to go."

I giggled. "Suddenly fucking Velma isn't as tempting as you thought it'd be?"

He let out a chuckle of his own, shaking his head. "Not when fucking Dezireé sounds so much better."

Well, gaaaahdamn. How was a girl supposed to say no to that?

She wasn't, which was exactly why I snatched that fucking

wig off my head faster than a bitch finna get her ass beat and tossed it across the room to give him what he asked for.

This time when he reached up, it was to undo the two thick braids I'd put my hair in and let my coils down in all their glory. Those thick fingers of his dove in, allowing him to get just enough of a grip to force my head back and pull a whimper from my lips.

Izaiah had me doing that a lot tonight, which was wild because I wasn't even a whimpering, weak-in-the-knees kind of girl. How many more times would I make that sound before the night was over?

Based on the feel of his heavy dick against my stomach, I was willing to bet a lot more. I didn't wait for him to initiate the kiss this time, needing to take the lead and leave my mark on him the way he'd seemingly marked me.

And when Izaiah groaned in response?

There was no way to describe the dip my stomach made, but goddamn I wouldn't mind feeling it again. It turned me on, knowing I was the one drawing that sound from him. He broke the kiss as his hands gave my ass a rough squeeze. This time, it was my turn to groan.

"Fuck, I wanted to do that shit from the moment I saw you in this skirt." The words were barely out of his mouth before he was picking me up and setting me on top of the washer.

"Look at you acting all big and strong," I giggled, leaning forward to kiss his neck. My teeth nipped at his skin and my tongue flicked out to soothe the exact same spot, earning me another appreciative groan. I loved a man who wasn't afraid to be vocal.

Show me how much you like that shit, daddy, so I can—

My thoughts came to a halt as his thumb traced over my hardened nipple through my shirt. I whined, wanting more.

Two points to me for not wearing a bra. It was becoming the new norm in Izaiah's presence.

"Are you sure about this?" His words were strained as I trailed kisses along his collarbone, but the message was clear. If I didn't want this to happen, it wouldn't.

My fingers pulled at the hem of his shirt. "Zay, I appreciate your dedication to getting my consent, I swear I do. It's very fucking sexy. But right now, the only thing I need you to do is take this shit off."

Instead of fighting me, he just gave me that signature lopsided smirk of his and did as I asked. Right now wasn't the time to contemplate a damn thing. The liquor had loosened both of our inhibitions, giving us the perfect excuse. Quite frankly I'd spent way too many nights, walls spasming around my fingers and moans falling from my lips, as I imagined his dick making me come over and over again. I'd be a fool not to take the opportunity to experience the real thing.

My hands made quick work of undoing his pants.

One of Izaiah's hands went to my throat, applying just enough pressure to pull a desperate, hungry sound out of me.

"If you take that out, you better act like you know what to do with it, Dezireé." I looked up at him with hooded eyes and what I saw made my pussy clench in anticipation. "I mean that shit."

Shit, so did I.

My hand slipped into his pants and found exactly what I was looking for, long, thick, and waiting.

"Mmm, mmm, mmm," I hummed as he shuddered against me. The size of him gave me an unimaginable craving.

If we'd had more time, I'd have dropped to my knees right then and there and used my mouth to worship what I just knew was probably the most beautiful dick I'd ever seen.

I almost said fuck it and did it anyway, but with the looming threat of someone from the party walking in on us, I ignored the urge. As I began to stroke him, the moans falling from his lips were music to my ears. The pressure against my neck increased as he kissed me again. How did he know I loved that type of shit real bad? This nigga was finna ruin me before he ever blessed me with an inch.

I was no stranger to sex, but this was on a whole other level. My pussy had never clenched with this much anticipation. I'd never had kisses that singed every bit of skin they touched. Never experienced the sharp intake of breath Izaiah was pulling from me as he bit my neck so hard that it wouldn't surprise me if he'd broken the skin. That shit alone turned me on so bad that barely a second went by before I was sure that I didn't give a fuck if he had or not.

Another whimper escaped my lips as Izaiah's tongue slid over my neck, stopping in various spots to deliver flicks that sent shock waves straight to my clit. His hands made their way down my body before returning to cup my breasts, grazing and pulling both nipples through my shirt. My head dropped back as I hissed.

"*Shiiit.*"

My eyes opened to the sight of him smirking down at me. Squinting, not wanting him to think he had the upper hand, I gave his dick a stroke before running my thumb across his precum-slicked tip. His hips bucked and his face pressed into the side of my neck.

"Fuck, Zee," he rasped. I couldn't help but laugh. "Oh, you think you funny, huh?"

I shrugged. "I might be." My smug attitude didn't last long.

In response, he made quick work of ripping my fishnets, his fingers lightly running along the seam of my covered lips, just barely applying any sort of pressure. I whined in frustration and lifted my hips, trying to force him to give me what I wanted.

"Now who's the funny one?" he asked with a chuckle.

"Come on, Zay. *Stop playing,*" I said with a pout.

"Do you promise to be a good girl?" He leaned down, sealing the question with a quick kiss.

I nodded and gave him another slow stroke as he moved my panties to the side. Cool air hit my wet lips, drawing a sharp gasp from my chest.

"Did you make this mess just for me?" His middle finger parted my lips and that first light touch against my clit caused my hips to buck.

My eyes drifted closed and a satisfied smile took over my face. My hips gave a small thrust, willing him to go deeper. He made sure not to disappoint, pushing two thick fingers into my warm, wet center.

"You feel that, Zee? You feel the way your shit is gripping me?"

If Izaiah was expecting a coherent answer, baby, he was going to be disappointed. The only thing I could manage to do was nod as I released his dick and gripped the washer, using the newfound leverage to rock my hips and meet each thrust of his fingers. When the palm of his hand put pressure on my already sensitive clit, I couldn't help the silence-piercing moan that escaped.

"*Fuuuck.*" I was trying but failing to keep my voice down. The music may have still been blasting upstairs, but I wasn't exactly prepared to test the theory that it was too loud for anyone to hear us.

As Izaiah leaned down and sucked a covered nipple into his mouth, my brain damn near short-circuited.

Yeah, I actually don't give a good goddamn who hears us.

No sooner had the thought crossed my mind did heat start to pool in the pit of my stomach. The type that could only mean one thing. My breath came in pants as my walls clenched.

"That's right, Zee, chase that shit. Take what you want," Izaiah whispered in my ear. "Let me feel you come."

His fingers bent in a come-here motion, grazing my g-spot. My body shook as I did just as he said, my moans echoing through the room. With each new wave of pleasure, his fingers never stopped moving, fucking me and rubbing my clit, extending my orgasm for as long as he possibly could until it finally came to an end.

Or at least I'd thought it was the end. He had other plans, sucking the sensitive place on my neck he'd found earlier. The move had me coming all over again, this time cursing up a storm.

Goddamn, this nigga was going to fucking ruin me.

I pushed him away just enough to get him to stop and look at me. Zay smirked, pulled his fingers out of my pussy, and brought one to his lips, sucking it hungrily.

Ruin. Me.

But why should he get to have all the fun?

I took his hand into mine, placing the second finger into my own mouth.

"How your ass got the nerve to be fine as hell and taste good as fuck all at the same time?" he asked as he watched me taste myself.

"Guess that's just one of the mysteries of life," I giggled. He smirked in response, pressing my lips to his and parting them until he was sucking on my tongue. Almost like he couldn't get enough of me.

CHAPTER
SEVEN

| IZAIAH |

"PLEASE TELL ME YOU HAVE A CONDOM."

My entire body froze as Deziree's words washed over me.

"Fuck!"

Her head dropped forward into my chest. "You cannot be serious right now."

"I didn't exactly plan this shit." Had I hoped to see her tonight? Yeah. That was half the reason my ass was even at this party. But I never actually thought we'd end up in *this* situation.

"You're literally a firefighter. Aren't y'all always supposed to be prepared?"

I couldn't help but chuckle even though there was nothing funny about this shit. "That's the Boy Scouts, baby girl."

"Same difference."

Not really, but I decided to let her have it if that's what it took to lighten the mood.

We stood in silence for what felt like a lifetime, watching each other. I didn't need for Deziree to tell me what she was thinking as she peeked up at me through hooded eyelids. Whatever it was had recklessness written all over it, just like the expression on her face.

I was proven right when she reached down, taking my dick in her hand again, never breaking eye contact.

"Zee," I warned, hardly recognizing the growl in my voice. My hips jerked forward as she began to stroke it. "Stop fucking playing with me right now."

"Who's playing?" She cocked her head to the side and leaned back to give me a full view of her.

"You 'cause why are you acting like you're still trying to get fucked?"

My eyes traced every move she made as she slid to the edge of the washer and lifted up just enough to get rid of her tights and draws before gripping me again and lining my dick up with her opening.

"Because I am."

Goddamn

"Baby girl..."

"I'm serious. My last test was four weeks ago and I haven't been with anyone in four months. Before that it was Matty and well...that was well over a year ago."

I leaned in, letting her hands guide my movements as her words sank in. "My last test was a few months ago, but I'm good too. I haven't been with anyone since..."

The calculations flashed quickly through my mind as I fought not to get distracted by the way her thumb was tracing over my tip. "Since November." Damn, had it really been eight months?

"Good. So now that we've done our due diligence as responsible adults..." Zee fluttered those big, beautiful eyes at me innocently. "Show me what it feels like to come on this pretty ass dick of yours."

Well, when she put it that way, how was I supposed to deny her what she wanted? What we both clearly wanted.

Fuck the consequences. We were grown and both well aware of what was happening despite the drinks we'd consumed.

Whatever little angel might have been trying to appear on my shoulder exited stage left, leaving behind a voice that said *slide into that wet ass pussy and don't look back.*

I made quick work of kicking my pants out the way and allowed myself to revel in the heat coming from between her thighs. There was no doubt in my mind that her pussy would be the perfect meal. I found myself wishing I could eat that shit off the bone. From the front, back, and side. We didn't have time for that right now, but I made sure to add it to my to-do-list for next time. And there would for damn sure be a next time because there was no way once would be enough. Nah, after tonight, baby girl was going to be my new addiction.

When I didn't immediately make a move, her face balled up in confusion. "What are you waiting for?"

So glad you asked.

Tangling one hand in her curls, I tilted her head back and placed a featherlight kiss against her lips.

"Put it in."

The words weren't a suggestion. Nah, they were an all-out demand. If Dezi;eé wanted this dick so fucking bad, she needed to show me she could be a big girl and take it all on her own.

Her eyes narrowed as she smacked her lips. "You know I hate it when a nigga tells me what to do."

"Unless he can tell you what to do," I shot back. I'd heard her say those exact words more times than I could count. There was no doubt in my mind that I was *that* nigga.

The attitude she'd just been ready to give me melted away. "Touché."

The smirk on my face began to falter as she slid my length into her heat, eyes never leaving mine. Or at least that would've been the case if the feel of her, warm and wet around me, hadn't made my own eyes snap shut.

Did it make me a bitch that my eyes immediately rolled back behind my lids as soon as I felt the first spasm of her walls around my dick?

Truth be told, I didn't give a fuck if it did. I'd gladly claim the title. Dezireé felt better than I could've ever imagined. It was pure gratification and torture all at the same fucking time.

Goddamn, was I even breathing? Did I want to be? I could die right here between her thighs and wouldn't give a shit. Matter of fact, whoever was in charge of my tombstone could write *Here lies Izaiah Price, the nigga who died the happiest man on earth,* and they'd be right.

"Perfection," I whispered against her lips, trying my hardest to give her time to adjust to my size despite the fact that every nerve ending I had was telling me to move. Apparently, she didn't give a fuck about my concern, something she made clear by the way she wiggled her hips.

"Feeling real impatient aren't you?" I slid out of her, slow and measured.

"You say impatient, I say horny."

With a raised eyebrow, my hips slammed back into hers with enough force that her breath hitched in her throat.

"Well, maybe we should see what we can do to fix that."

My tight grip on her hips kept her steady as I filled her over and over again. Each stroke sent a shock wave of pleasure through my body, and hers too if the moans falling from her lips were any indication.

Why had it taken us so damn long to do this? For the life of me, I couldn't remember.

If I had known her pussy was this fucking good...

The shit was surreal. Here I was, digging her out on top of her best friend's washer in a house full of people, and not only was she letting me, she was fucking me back. Shit, I was ready to beg her to let me do it again and we weren't even finished the first go round yet.

As I struggled to keep my composure, she reached up and grabbed the back of my neck, holding on for dear life as my right hand left her hip and reached into her shirt. I couldn't resist the urge to roll her nipple between my fingers.

"Oooh," she whined, arching into my touch. "Why would you be fu-fucking me like th-this? It's n-not r-right."

"Fucking you like what?" I grunted, my brow knitted in concentration. Leaning down, my hand moved from her chest to her neck, gripping it to pull her in for another hungry kiss. A kiss that was so nasty I could've sworn it made her pussy even wetter.

"Like you own this shit," she gasped when the kiss finally ended.

Whether it was the words or the feel of her, I wasn't sure, but I groaned in response, deepening my stroke.

"'Cause after tonight, Zee, this is *my* pussy. Why else would I be writing my name all over it?"

CHAPTER
EIGHT

| DEZIREÉ |

AIN'T *no way this nigga really just said that shit.*

I wanted to argue. Wanted to hit him with some slick remark, but as I barreled toward my second orgasm of the night, I couldn't focus long enough to form the words.

He was fucking me like he wanted me obsessed, and based on how much I was dripping all over his dick, I was well on my way.

Izaiah's name flowed out of me as he let my neck go, first in pants and whispers, only to turn into full-on cries of pleasure sounding through the entire basement. If anyone really did decide to come looking for us, they were in for one hell of a show.

"You feel so goddamn good wrapped around my dick, baby girl. Look at what you're doing to me."

It took everything I had in me to follow his directions, but when my eyes finally opened—*and when the fuck had they closed in the first place?*—the sight of his dick coated in my juices was so fucking erotic I couldn't help myself.

"*Shiiiit*, I'm coming. Zay, I'm coming."

My new favorite hand necklace tightened as I leaned back completely, body shaking from the power of his thrusts as I struggled to find purchase against the cold surface of the washer.

It felt like I was on another planet. Where was I and how did I stay here?

My walls tightened as I began to ramble. Was it my imagination or had I just told this man to never stop fucking me?

I must have because even as my orgasm began to wane, his strokes didn't. Our hips came together in constant motion as if our bodies were trying to see who would break first. Considering Izaiah already had me headed toward my third nut of the night, it was safe to say it would probably be me.

But I'm taking his good dick-having ass with me if it's the last thing I do.

"Dezireé…"

With his body leaned into mine, his mouth was right next to my ear. The sound of him moaning my name? Goddamn, had anything ever been that fucking sexy?

"Pussy must be too good if it's got you whimpering like that." When he only grunted in response, I couldn't help but giggle as I circled my hips, meeting each of his thrusts.

"Oh, you think you cute, huh?"

"Oh, Zay, I don't think. I know."

One hand moved between our bodies and the moment he made contact with my clit, waves of ecstasy shot through me.

"*Ahhh, shit.*" My pussy spasmed, sucking him in deeper.

"How did I stay away from this shit for so long?"

Was he asking himself or did he expect me to answer? I had no idea because the way Zay wrapped his arms around me and slowed his strokes down, digging in deeper, made it impossible to focus.

This nigga really got some audacity fucking me like this.

His tongue slid over my neck as he added, "It's like goddamn paradise, Zee."

A motherfucking word cause the dick was so good, I could feel my toes throwing up gang signs. My fingernails dug into his neck as I bit down on my lip hard enough to draw blood, trying to muffle my moans.

"Let that shit out, baby. Let me know how it feels," he said, his hands no longer around my back but gripping my thighs as he pulled me even closer.

"Fucking amazing. That's how it feels." He gave my thighs another squeeze and I choked out a moan so loud that it seemed to fill the entire basement. "*Oooh fuck!*"

We stayed like that, bodies tangled together, moans topping one another until I felt my legs begin to shake and my walls started to clench around him.

"I need... I ne—" I could barely get the words out.

"Tell me what you need, Zee."

"Faster," I moaned. "*Fuuuck*, I'm gonna come. Fuck me faster."

That was all he needed to hear to send him into overdrive as he leaned up and began delivering his strokes at a merciless pace. The combination of his forceful thrusts and his thumb circling my clit set me off like fireworks. I opened my mouth to scream, but his lips met mine in a kiss that both swallowed my moans and mixed them with his own sounds of pleasure.

Trapped in a never-ending earthquake, my vision blurred, forcing me to shut my eyes. Izaiah wasn't far behind me and before long, his cum was coating my walls, each warm rope causing a flurry of aftershocks.

When his body finally relaxed, he was still holding me close, though his grip had eased up. We stayed like that, both trying to catch our breaths as we came down from our mutual high. I placed soft, lazy kisses along his jawline as we settled, ones he accepted without complaint.

I was the first to hear the elevated music as if the door to the basement was opened. The creak of the top step made it painfully clear it had been.

Shit. I guess neither of us had been smart enough to lock the door. We were stuck, frozen in place, me half-naked on top of a major appliance and Izaiah's soft dick still buried deep inside of me.

"Aye, Zay, you down there?"

I knew that voice. I grew up with that voice. By the look he was giving me, Izaiah recognized it too.

Grayson.

I buried my face in the crook of his neck, praying my brother couldn't see me. I was pretty sure the laundry area wasn't visible from the steps as long as you didn't go beyond the top three or so, but fucking hell, shit was going to get a lot worse if he decided to actually come downstairs.

"Uh, yeah, I'm down here."

What the hell?

I pulled back enough to shoot him a look that told him to shut up.

"I'm kinda busy, Gray. What's up?" He was trying to keep his voice steady and calm as if he hadn't just finished fucking the sense out of me.

"Yeah, I'm sure." We heard my brother chuckle knowingly. At least he *thought* he knew what was going on. "Listen, I don't mean to interrupt, but if you plan on catching a ride with me, you better stop being busy in about five minutes. Unless you got another way home."

Zay looked at me with a question in his eyes. I shook my head and tried to ignore the disappointment there. That wasn't a good idea and not just because I planned to stay here for the night. After a brief pause, Izaiah called out, "A'ight, I got you. I'll be up in a minute."

I held my breath and waited until we heard the door shut. "That was close."

"Yeah…I know," he said, his eyes meeting mine before they darted away. "Guess maybe the shit wasn't as good for you as I thought if I can't even get a ride." The words were said as a joke, but the hurt behind them was plain as day.

He slid out of me, and as soon as he did, I could feel his cum following suit. Why did that leave me turned on?

"It's not that. Trust me. Definitely ten out of ten over here. No notes," I said with what I hoped was a reassuring smile. "But I'm not exactly going home tonight. Trina and I are staying over so we can do a birthday brunch with Kamille in the morning."

"And if you weren't? Staying, I mean," he asked as I slid off the washer and used my panties to clean myself up before tossing both them and the fishnets in a nearby trash can.

"Oh, I'd definitely be taking you home with me for round two…and three."

Izaiah chuckled as he got himself together. "Happy to hear you're a satisfied customer. Be sure to leave a glowing review and tip your server."

This nigga.

"Here's a tip for you," I said, coming in close and wrapping my arms around his neck. "Next time, let me swallow. Wouldn't want my throat getting jealous of my pussy now, would we?"

Shaking his head, he placed his hands on my waist. "You're some kinda nasty, you know that?"

There was nothing for me to do except shrug because since when was that a bad thing?

"Guess I better get started on my walk of shame, huh?"

"Mmhmm, you better," I teased.

He smirked and pulled me in for a kiss that made me want to say fuck the sleepover and the brunch.

Displaying a lot more willpower than I clearly had, Izaiah broke the kiss, leaving me with a smile and a palpitating heart as he jogged up the steps.

It was only a few seconds before I heard the door open and close behind him.

That man had officially left me freshly fucked, satisfied, utterly alone and craving a repeat performance.

CHAPTER
NINE

| DEZIREÉ |

THE HANGOVER TORMENTING me the next day was a reminder that I was too goddamn old to be drinking like a college undergrad. I couldn't even remember drinking that mu—

Oh, right.

After having the best sex of my life, I'd managed to sneak back upstairs just in time to see Izaiah heading out the door with Grayson. That was also around the time Kamille spotted me and immediately demanded I be her tequila pong partner because apparently, Trina was nowhere to be found.

"Where is Matt? You know he's better at this than any of us."

"I sent him off to find Trina like fifteen minutes ago and haven't seen either of them since. She blew up on my neighbor because his ass stepped on her foot." She gave me a look. *"She almost took his head off until I convinced her to go cool*

down. But they never came back. I swear if my friends keep disappearing like this, I'm going to develop a complex."

At least it was backing up my best friend that got me drunk off my ass and not what I'd done with Izaiah.

I swear I could still feel the ache between my thighs from the way he'd fucked me. That man had sent me to another stratosphere and I just let him walk up out of here...*alone.* What the fuck was I thinking? He was a danger to society walking around with all that good dick.

If I'd been thinking with my pussy the way I should have been, we would've left together, sleepover plans be damned. I deserved a fucking medal because I just know if we'd made it home, he would've put me through the mattress.

If only.

Just the thought of what could have been had me clenching my thighs for relief. Everything was coming back to me in flashes.

The feel of his hands gripping my waist.

The taste of his tongue.

Shit, the way his strokes hit just the right angle, tapping against my—

"Too goddamn good."

"Giiiirl," a voice grumbled next to me. By the sound of her voice, Kamille was still very much asleep and ready to kill my ass for ruining that. "Can you please shut your loud ass up?"

I couldn't help but laugh. "Kami, I'm barely making any noise." I was so busy cracking up that there was no time to block the pillow she sent flying at my face.

"Rude!" Looking around, I added, "What are you even doing in here? Couldn't make it to your own bed last night?"

"First of all, all the beds in this house belong to me."

I rolled my eyes as she stretched.

"Second, after you passed out last night—a full hour before people started leaving, I might add—somebody had to come check on your drunk ass." Kamille's brow furrowed as she finally sat up. "You know, you're way more of a lightweight than you used to be."

"Or I had no business playing that damn game with you, especially since you can't shoot for shit."

"*Anywaaay*," she started, quick to skip over that little fact, "I came to check on you and may or may not have been too drunk to make it the last few steps to my own room."

"Of course you were."

We really were two peas in a pod.

"Did you ever find Trina?"

"Like did I actually see her? No. I did eventually find Matt, though, and he said she was good, so…" She shrugged. "But while we're talking about disappearing acts, where the hell did your ass go last night?"

"Didn't you ask me that last night?"

"I did, and you deflected then *just* like you're doing right now." Kamille's eyes narrowed with suspicion. "Your ass is so transparent I can see right through you."

"And you are a literal pain in the ass. We all have our crosses to bear. Now get up. I'm starving and I believe someone was promised a catered brunch."

"Yeah…me," she said, a smile lighting up her face.

Since she'd taken care of her own party, Trina and I organized a private chef to come in and do brunch with all her favorites. A chef who should be arriving right about now if that clock was correct.

The doorbell chimed right on time.

"You get your ass in the shower and I'll go answer that."

"Don't have to tell me twice." Kamille pushed away the comforter and climbed out of bed. While she handled her business, I quickly went to let the chef in and show her where she could set up. Then it was time to find the missing member of our trio.

"I was wondering how long it would take one of y'all to come get on my nerves." In true Trina fashion, she said the words without ever looking up from her Kindle.

"Whatcha reading?" I asked, sliding into bed next to her.

"*Rhythm's Blues* by Kimberly Brown. Baby girl just unknowingly got bent over by her ex-boyfriend's producer and I am *living*."

"Not you in your forbidden romance bag."

"It's not my fault shit feels sweeter when you're not supposed to want it."

A look came across her face—one I knew all too well, especially after last night. Now who exactly had caught my girl's eye?

"Speaking from experience?"

Trina quickly schooled her expression as she put the Kindle down. "Now you know better than that," she said, and I swear her chuckle sounded nervous.

"Mmm, maybe not 'cause your ass is jittery as fuck right now."

"Only because you came in here disrupting my peace."

"Mhmm...or because you snuck off last night without a word."

"You're one to talk."

Okay, she had me there.

"So are we going to talk about who you were off with or..."

"Noooo, we're going to both get ready 'cause the chef is here and I know your ass is just as hungry as the rest of us." I was going to try and avoid this conversation as long as I could.

"That's what I thought," she giggled.

Finding my way right to the exit, I decided to give my bestie a reprieve, at least for now. Whatever she was hiding would come out eventually.

But probably not before my situation with Izaiah.

One hour, three showers, and three matching pajamas later, we were all practically devouring the spread the chef had put together.

"Oh my gosh, Chef Indigo, if I could, I think I'd swim in this hot honey maple syrup," Kamille said as she danced in her chair.

The gorgeous woman who was just about finished cleaning the kitchen laughed.

"I want you to know she's very serious. Leave enough of that stuff behind and she'll probably be a sticky mess later," I said.

"I'm just glad y'all are enjoying everything. And please, call me Indie."

"Baby, the way these Key lime waffles taste, I'll call you whatever you want me to."

She'd really gone full out. Veggie frittatas, fried chicken, Key lime waffles, peach cobbler French toast, and Cajun salmon over Gouda grits? No wonder her schedule was always booked and busy if this was the type of shit she was slinging.

After assuring her that we could deal with the leftovers if there even were any, Indie let herself out, leaving us to our own devices. My aversion to alcohol had disappeared because it seemed nothing was going to keep me from enjoying the mango pineapple mimosas she'd put together.

"I have to hand it to you, Kamille. You outdid yourself last night," Trina said before taking another bite. "And we finna be drained as hell cleaning all this up."

I snickered. "You know damn well your friend hired a cleaning service for that."

"And did," Kami cackled. "They'll be here in a few hours, but until then, we have the place all to ourselves." She did a little shimmy in her seat. "But seriously, though, last night might've been my best party yet. Shit, I hope y'all enjoyed it cause they may be canceled until further notice. I mean, how am I supposed to top myself after that?"

Trina and I couldn't stop ourselves from rolling our eyes. Kamille said the same shit every year.

"When are you going to stop spouting that same tired ass line?"

"I really mean it this time, y'all!"

"Of course, you do, sweetie," Trina said, reaching across to pat her lightly on the arm. That sent me into a fit of laughter and it wasn't long before Trina was joining me.

"Hating ass hoes," Kamille mumbled, but there was no mistaking the smirk tugging at the edge of her lips. "I'm surprised you even noticed how much fun it was since you disappeared for the last couple hours, Ms. Trina. So tell me, who were you doing?"

Funny how interesting her plate was now that she'd been called out. "Girl, please. I felt sick, so I went to lay down and just fell asleep. That's it."

"You expect us to believe the queen of party shots couldn't hang and tapped out early?"

"Yep because that's what happened."

"More like she was getting tapped," I said under my breath. When two pairs of eyes snapped in my direction, I knew I'd fucked up.

Just couldn't keep your mouth shut, could you, bitch?

"Speaking of tapped, where did you carry your ass to?"

I nearly choked on a piece of chicken at Kamille's question. "Huh?" I asked.

"If you can huh, you can hear," she said, kicking up an eyebrow.

Trina didn't hesitate to jump in, happy the heat was off of herself. "Last I saw, she was taking her fast ass down to the basement."

Traitor!

"I just needed a break."

"You needed *a break* or needed someone to *break you off?*"

Now it was their turn to cackle together. They made me sick.

"Y'all are annoying as fuck."

"That doesn't change the fact that I definitely saw you leading Zay down them steps like you had his nose wide ass open."

Kamille gasped as I dropped my fork and groaned.

"Now see, I was just playing. Friend, do not tell me you took that man downstairs and fucked him in my basement."

Well... "More like he fucked the shit out of me in your basement," I finally confessed. No point in hiding what happened from my girls. Besides, *someone* had to know about the full-service dick I'd gotten.

"Biiitch! And it took you this long to say something? You ain't shit!" squealed Kamille.

"I mean damn, y'all act like you already know all my business so I'm surprised you need me to say anything at all."

"Girl, fuck all that! You really got the dick? With your brother and your ex right upstairs?" Trina leaned in, her own drama forgotten.

"Mmhmm…"

"And it was…?"

I sighed as an image came back to me. "If the dick could talk —and I'm not convinced it can't—I'd have a full conversation with his shit about how I'd let it ruin my life."

"I know you lying," they said in unison.

"Baby, life, career goals, credit, my walls, all that shit."

We all paused before bursting into laughter. They thought I was joking, but shit was something serious.

"I guess you meant it when you said Matty was in the past." A thoughtful expression crossed Trina's face. There wasn't much time to analyze it because Kamille cut in.

"Hold up. Where exactly did you have this life-changing dick?"

I mumbled my response, but clearly not low enough.

"My washing machine? Really, Dezireé?!" She made a gagging sound.

"Girl, don't be so dramatic," I giggled.

"Your ass needs to worry less about my dramatics and more about sanitizing my shit! I hope you cleaned up after yourself because I don't think I signed off on you bussin' it wide open in the same place I wash my draws." Kamille scrunched up her face. "The only person supposed to be getting bent over in here is me."

"Then I guess you've got some catching up to do."

CHAPTER
TEN

| IZAIAH |

THE OTHER NIGHT was already permanently ingrained in my mind. Nothing about the way it played out was like I'd imagined.

I mean yeah, okay, I'd gone hoping that I'd get to chill with Dezireé, or at the very least see her. What I didn't count on was how much being around her in that environment would tempt the fuck out of me. Lights low, liquor flowing, and her looking sexy as fuck in her costume? Baby girl had worked out the recipe to my downfall and didn't even know it.

While the whole thing left its mark on me, it was the way she looked, lips tucked between her teeth and her brow furrowed in ecstasy and concentration right before she came, that really stuck.

Her whimpers.

The way it felt being inside of her. I swear the feel of her wrapped around my dick was just...*goddamn*.

It was enough to drive me up the fucking wall. I'd never been with a woman like Deziréé and I knew without a doubt it was because there was no other woman like her.

"Nigga, are you even listening?" Grayson asked, giving me a shove.

Hell no. I hadn't heard a damn thing he'd said.

"My bad, bruh, just zoned out for a sec." I rubbed the back of my neck and chuckled.

Pull yourself together.

It was either that or explain to my best friend and the other niggas on shift why I was fucking drooling with a hard ass dick in the middle of the station.

"Didn't you say this nigga disappeared during the party y'all went to? He's probably thinking about whoever he slipped away with," Jax, one of our shift mates, snickered.

Was his ass psychic or was I just that fucking transparent?

"You're just mad 'cause your ass was left out...again," I shot back.

"Not at all. I took my lil' shorty to see that new animated movie Sugar Hill Studios just put out. His ass had a blast."

I couldn't even clown him 'cause I knew how seriously he took that dad shit. Hearing that he and his son had spent some quality time together, especially after how stressful our last shift was, warmed my heart, no bullshit.

"Yeah, yeah, yeah. We all know you're Father of the Year, my nigga. Now how about you go be EMT of the Year and make sure the inventory in the unit is ready for whatever shit this shift throws our way?"

Jax didn't need to be told twice. He headed off to take care of that task and I guess everyone else took that as their cue to disperse as well, leaving me and Grayson alone.

After about sixty seconds of silence, he finally said, "So you gonna come clean or what?"

Come clean?

"Fuck you talking about?"

"About who you were in the basement with. And before you even think about lying, you should probably know that I went looking for Dezi's ass to see if she'd seen you. Considering y'all were both MIA, it doesn't take a genius to put two and two together."

It was a miracle my jaw wasn't on the damn floor.

The smirk on his face was devious as fuck and quickly turned annoying once he started to laugh. "Nigga, you should see yourself!" he said as he wiped a stray tear from his cheek.

"What is so fucking funny?" Was I irritated? Yes. But at least my shoulders didn't feel so fucking tense anymore.

"You, and the fact that y'all really thought the two of you got away with some shit."

"Nobody was trying to get away with anything." My defensive tone only made him snicker that much harder.

"Sure, whatever you say." He paused. "Then again, maybe you're telling the truth since it was so obvious. I'm just glad you finally stepped the fuck up because the way you were drooling over her ass was actually pitiful."

"So you just think you know every fucking thing, huh?"

"Nah, I don't, and trust me, I don't want to. You can keep the nasty ass details to yourself."

I wasn't sure if the disgusted shiver he gave was real or an act, but I shook my head either way.

"But I do know the two of you have been playing this little cat and mouse game for too damn long, so thank you for putting us all out of our misery."

Grayson made his way to the oven just as it beeped to let us know that lasagna was ready. We all typically took turns making shift meal and it was his, which everyone was anticipating. Grayson might have been irritating as a fucking mosquito, but the man knew how to get down in the kitchen.

Honestly, I didn't even know what to say or do at this point. I mean, I figured someone could have noticed the fact that we disappeared, but Gray being the one to do it? Yeah, not what I was expecting or hoping for.

"You gonna just stand there scratching your head or grab the garlic bread before it burns?"

Usually I'd give him shit about his smart ass mouth, but instead I just got started with the task at hand. Finally, after putting the garlic bread on the table and grabbing the salad out the fridge, I decided on a response.

"Are you okay with this, Gray? I mean for real. No bullshit."

I didn't need to ask for my best friend's permission to pursue his sister. We were all too grown for that. Even still, having his blessing would at least put my mind at ease and keep things from getting awkward, both personally and professionally.

Luckily, he agreed with the former.

"Zay, I appreciate the concern 'cause you're my homeboy and all, but what the fuck I look like trying to tell two grown ass adults what to do? That would be some weak ass shit on my part, and I ain't a weak ass nigga. Who y'all decide to start fuckin' with is not my business, even if it happens to be each other."

The rest of the crew made their way into the kitchen, adding noise to the otherwise silent area. Grayson leaned in, closing the distance between us.

"And the only way I'll ever make it my business is if you show your ass and disrespect her. You may be my nigga, but that's my sister. She'll always come first."

I nodded in understanding because if he hadn't added that last part, then he wasn't really the man I thought he was.

"So we're good?" One more bit of reassurance wouldn't hurt.

"For sure. Shit, your ass was already half sprung before. I can only imagine the type of sick little puppy you're about to be now. I'm pretty sure it'll make for a good show."

He dodged the dry dish towel I tossed at his head.

"Not you trying to figure your brother-in-law already? Yep, she's about to have your nose wide ass open."

I grumbled for him to shut up as everyone began making their plates. Funny thing was, as I took out my phone, I couldn't even pretend like he wasn't right.

IZAIAH:

You busy tomorrow night?

DEZIREÉ:

I might have plans…

IZAIAH:

Change 'em. I'll make it worth your while.

DEZIREÉ:

You better 😊

Lucky for both of us, I was a man of my word.

The end...for now.

A FINAL WORD

I've been wanting to tell Dezi and Izaiah's story for years and that's not an exaggeration. Their tale has changed shape several times, but in the end this felt the most authentic. I hope they were worth the wait.

If you're able, please find the time to leave a rating and/or review on your favorite platform (Goodreads, Storygraph, etc.). They're the best way to help readers find new favorites and so important when supporting indie authors.

To keep up-to-date on upcoming Lady Marie projects, be sure to sign up for the Spice In Your Life Newsletter, join me on Patreon (Lady Marie Affair), check out my linktree, and follow me on social media @ladymariewrites.

To order a signed copy of any of my physical projects, merch, or web exclusives, please visit the Lady Marie Shop at lady mariewrites.com

ALSO BY LADY MARIE

SISTERS & SERENDIPITY SERIES

Worth It (A Fake Dating Novel)

Found Forever (An Established Couple, After the HEA Novella)

SUGARED AND SPICED SERIES

Sugar, Sugar (An Age Gap, Sugar Arrangement Novella)

Sweet Heat (A FFM Age Gap, Sugar Arrangement Novella)

Sugar-Coated Kisses (An Age Gap Insta-love Novella)

Sweet Control (An Age Gap, Sugar Arrangement Novella)

SLEIGH THE NIGHT COLLECTION

After Tonight (A Brother's Best Friend Novella, _Sleigh the Night_ Prequel)

Sleigh the Night (A Winter Shorts Collection)

HOLIDAY NOVELLAS AND SHORT STORIES

With Sugar on Top (A Sugared and Spiced NYE Short)

Sinnamon & Golds (A Lick Back Season, Thanksgiving Novella)

Szn's Greetings (A Sinnamon & Golds Christmas Short)

Resolutions (A New Year's Novellette)